MARCUS SEDGWICK
CUDWEED'S
TIME MACHINE

Illustrated by Pete Williamson

Orion
Children's Books

First published in Great Britain in 2013
by Orion Children's Books
a division of the Orion Publishing Group Ltd
Orion House
5 Upper St Martin's Lane
London WC2H 9EA
An Hachette UK Company

1 3 5 7 9 10 8 6 4 2

A catalogue record for this book is available from the British Library.

ISBN 978 1 4440 0484 7

Printed in China

www.orionbooks.co.uk
www.ravenmysteries.co.uk

For Pete's sake (Marcus Sedgwick)

For the Scott family (Pete Williamson)

CONTENTS

CHAPTER 1

This is Cudweed.

If you think *he* looks funny, you should see his mum

and his dad.

He has a big sister too, and she looks
like this, almost normal.

Almost.

If you think they all look a bit odd, you'd be right, but then, this is where they live.

And you couldn't live in a crazy castle like that and be normal, could you?

It's the sort of place where **odd** and **strange** things happen. A lot.
This is the story of what happened when Cudweed played with one of his dad's strange inventions…

Cudweed's dad is an inventor. Or he likes to think he is.

But he's not very good at it, and most of the time his inventions don't work.

Even when they *do* work, they are very silly. Once he invented invisible spoons, which made eating soup hard.

Then there was the machine that painted four walls at once.

And the boat made of toast. It would
have worked except that the fish in
the lake really seemed to like toast.

One day after lunch, Cudweed was thinking that it was a long time to wait until tea. He was bored, and he and his pet monkey Fellah went to look in the lab where his dad worked.

His dad wasn't there, but sitting in the middle of the floor was an amazing THING.

It looked like this:

It looked very exciting. It looked like something that Cudweed would like to mess about with.

He saw two words on the control
panel. The words were; TIME, and
MACHINE.

Cudweed read them slowly and
carefully, and then he looked at
Fellah, who was tugging at handles
and poking his fingers into sockets.

'I think it's a time machine…'
Cudweed said. 'Do you know, Fellah,
I've had an idea. If Dad has actually
built a time machine, we can use it.'

Fellah looked at him, then began
tugging levers again.

'Yes,' said Cudweed. 'We can use it to travel through time! To go forward! To tea-time! We won't have to wait! Brilliant!'

He climbed into the machine.

'I wonder how it works… Fellah,
get in and put on your seat belt. I've
never driven a time machine before.
Now…'

Cudweed looked at the controls, turned a few dials, flicked a few switches, and pushed a big green button that said '**GO**.'

'Tea-time here we come!' he cried.
There was a flash of light and a funny
fizzing sound.

When it stopped, Cudweed looked
around.

A lot of Roman soldiers were frowning
at him.

'Coo,' said Cudweed. 'I'm not sure
this is tea-time, after all.'

CHAPTER 2

Cudweed was right. They were no longer in the lab, but in a big sandy place.

A lot of Roman soldiers were staring at them. Behind them were some lions and tigers. And behind them was a large, noisy crowd.

The crowd was shouting, and what
they were shouting wasn't very nice.

The soldiers looked angry.

'I think,' Cudweed said to Fellah,
'that these are not Roman soldiers.
They are gladiators, and I think they
think that they're going to fight us.'
He gulped.
'Which is not a good idea. At all.'

The gladiators had sharp swords and nets, and long pointy fork things. They were coming towards Cudweed and Fellah.

'I might just push the **GO** button again, Fellah,' Cudweed said, quietly, 'if that's all right with you?'

As it happened, he didn't wait for Fellah to agree. Cudweed pushed the button.

Just in time, because as the flash of light and fizzing sound happened again, Cudweed heard a sword swish through the air right above their heads.

'Eek!' wailed Cudweed.

Fellah screeched.

They shut their eyes, but when they opened them again things were quite different.

Everything looked much safer.
No swords. No lions.
No screaming crowd.

Just green hills, with a forest not too far away. It was a sunny day, birds were flying in the sky and singing in the tree-tops.

'Phew!' said Cudweed. 'Where are we? Well, you know, I didn't think Dad could invent a machine that worked. But it seems like he has! Coo! A working time machine. Now all we need to do is to work out how to get to tea-time.'

He looked at the controls and found some buttons he had not seen before.

Fellah made a funny noise.
It sounded a bit as if he was being
strangled.

'Shh!' said Cudweed. 'Not now. I'm
thinking…'

Fellah made another funny noise.

'Fellah! Shh!' said Cudweed, sounding cross. 'I am really trying to think.'

Fellah made another noise, and this noise was so loud and odd and scary, that Cudweed looked up.

'Oh,' said Cudweed. 'I see.'

He'd seen what Fellah had seen.

Three very large and very hungry-looking dinosaurs charging towards them.

Cudweed wailed, and pushed the big **GO** button again.

And not a moment too soon, because one of the dinosaurs got close enough to bite the long pointy bit off the top of the time machine.

CHAPTER 3

Once again, there was a flash of light and a funny fizzing, and they disappeared.

They shut their eyes, and when they opened them, they had escaped from the dinosaurs.

Cudweed looked at the top of the machine.
'I hope it works without that pointy bit,' he said.

He sounded worried.

'Fellah,' he said. 'Why is the ground moving?'

Cudweed looked up and saw lots of things at once.

They weren't on land, but on a big boat. A ship. The ship had one square sail and a tall mast. At the front, it had a dragon's head.

Standing not too far away were some very tall men wearing furs and iron helmets.

There were many more of them rowing with long oars that stuck out on either side of the ship.

'Ulp,' said Cudweed. 'Fellah. I think we should get out of here. Unless I'm wrong, this is a Viking ship. And if I remember one thing about Vikings, it's that they like a good fight.'

Fellah hopped about looking worried.

Cudweed pushed the **GO** button again, and shut his eyes, waiting for the flash and the fizzing.

Nothing happened.

'Oh dear,' said Cudweed. 'Maybe that pointy bit was important after all. At least they haven't seen us yet.'

Then one of the Vikings turned and pointed at Cudweed and Fellah. '**Raaar!**' he said, or something like that.

The other Vikings turned too and they said, '**Raaar! Gaaar! Raaar-gaaaar!**'

They started to wave their swords and spears.

Fellah screeched, and shot up the mast as fast as if his tail was on fire.

The Vikings surrounded Cudweed.

The Viking chief bent down, peering at Cudweed with a mix of anger and confusion on his face.

'**Raaar?**' he barked at Cudweed.

'Coo,' said Cudweed. 'I'm really sure I don't speak Viking. I wish I did, because then I might be able to understand you.'

The Viking chief waved his sword under Cudweed's nose.

'**Raaar!**' he roared. Then he pointed at Cudweed. Then he pointed at the sea.

'But I think I understand you quite
well. You'd rather I left the boat,
yes?'

'**Raar!**' said the chief.

'Oh,' said Cudweed, 'I was afraid of
that.'

CHAPTER 4

Things were looking bad for Cudweed. The Vikings were about to make him jump off the ship.

When Fellah saw what was happening he was upset. He dropped from the top of the mast onto the Viking chief's head and banged on his helmet.

Then he began hopping about and leaping up and down and banging on all their helmets, until they were very cross.

They tried to catch him but he was too fast. Soon there was complete chaos on the ship.

'**Raaar!**' screamed the Vikings, and they all ran around after Fellah.

Cudweed realised that they had forgotten about him. And more than that, he was thinking something.

He had noticed that the spears the Vikings were carrying looked like the pointy bit of the time machine, the bit that the dinosaur had bitten off.

And there was one of the spears leaning against the mast.

Cudweed looked at the spear. He looked at the time machine.

Then, while all the Vikings were chasing Fellah, he picked up the spear and shoved it in place of the missing bit of the time machine.

The machine made a happy humming sound.

'Fellah!' cried Cudweed. 'Come here! It's time to go!'

Fellah didn't need telling again.
He jumped into Cudweed's lap and
Cudweed hit the big green **GO**
button.

There was that flash and fizz, and suddenly, when they opened their eyes, they were back home in the castle.

Cudweed and Fellah scampered into the dining room.

'Oh, Cudweed!' said Solstice. 'We were worried about you. Where were you? It's not like you to miss tea-time!'

Cudweed looked very bothered.
'Miss tea-time?' he repeated. 'Miss
tea-time?'

Solstice nodded.
'Yes, and there was really good
chocolate cake too.'

Cudweed looked upset, but then he
cheered up.
'Oh well,' he said. 'I'll just be going
then.'
He left the room, with Fellah
following him.

'I think I know how to work this now,' he said to Fellah, looking at the time machine again.

There was a flash and a fizz, and a moment or so later, Cudweed and Fellah walked into the dining room.

Solstice saw them first.
'Oh, Cudweed!' she cried. 'We were worried about you. It's nearly time for tea! And there's some lovely looking chocolate cake!'

'I know,' said Cudweed, and, helping himself to a large slice, he winked at Fellah.

What are you going to read next?

More adventures with Horrid Henry,

or go exploring with Shumba,

and brave the Jungle

and Arctic with Algy.

Find a frog prince with Tulsa

Also by Marcus Sedgwick

Cudweed's Birthday
Cudweed in Outer Space

or even a big, yellow, whiskery

Lion in the Meadow!

Tuck into some

Blood, Guts and
Rats' Tail Pizza,

learn to dance with
Sophie,

travel back
in time with

Cudweed

and sail away in

Noah's Ark.

Enjoy all the Early Readers.